The Logbook of the *Timandra*

Dear Reader

For thousands of years, people have moved from place to place, in search of a better life for themselves and their families.

Countries such as the USA, Canada, Australia and New Zealand all have diverse cultures and societies, built upon a history of emigration from other places.

... A NASTY HEAD SEA, SHIP PITCHING HEAVILY. ALL THE EMIGRANTS BELOW DECK BEING SEASICK ...

In this book, we can read first-hand accounts from the captain and passengers of an emigrant ship, the *Timandra*, which carried emigrants from England to New Zealand in 1841.

I hope you enjoy their stories!

John Parsons

My sincere thanks to the following people for their time, information, images and enthusiasm for this book:

Puke Ariki Museum and Library, New Plymouth District Council

National Library of New Zealand Te Puna Mātauranga o Aotearoa

Archives New Zealand Te Rua Mahara o te Kāwanatanga

NELSON
A Cengage Company

Contents

The Logbook of the *Timandra*

A

LOG-BOOK,

CONTAINING

THE PROCEEDINGS

ON BOARD THE

Timandra

From the Port of London

To New Plymouth New Zealand

COMMANDED BY

Commencing

Ending

KEPT BY

London:

Printed for and Sold by M. Watson, Jun. Bookseller, Stationer and Chartseller,

At the Navigation Warehouse, 360, Wapping High Street.

Index and Glossary page 32

1 Countdown to the Colonisation of New Zealand

1642

A **New** Land

In 1642, the Māori tribes who lived in Aotearoa had their first contact with Europeans. A Dutch explorer, Abel Tasman, and his two ships, the *Heemskerck* and the *Zeehaen*, anchored near the northern end of the South Island. Things didn't get off to a good start.

The next morning, Māori who lived in the area sent out canoes to investigate the new arrivals. A fight started and several men lost their lives. Tasman sailed away without landing.

A few years later, maps made of his voyage called the new land after a Dutch province: *Nieuw Zeeland*.

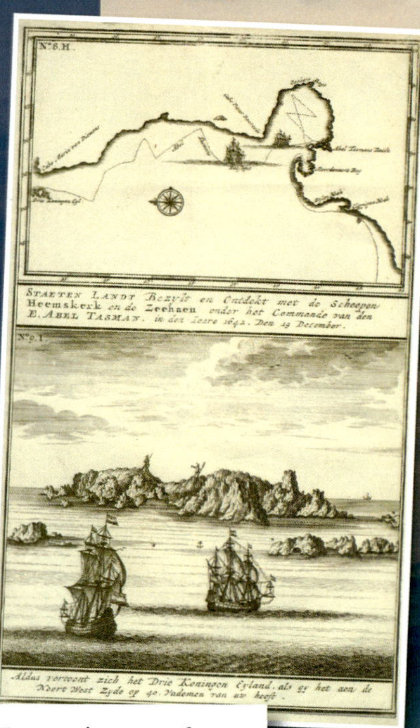

Abel Tasman's map of New Zealand and his two ships

AOTEAROA

The Māori name for New Zealand is Aotearoa, which means "land of the long white cloud".

Geography

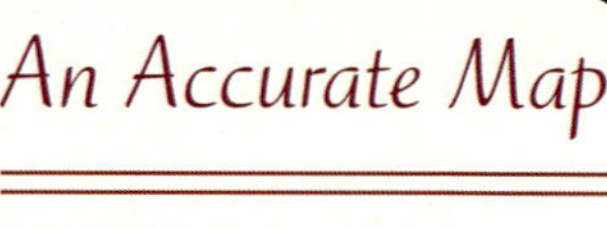

An Accurate Map

Abel Tasman's hand-drawn map of the north-western tip of the South Island was very accurate.

From 1642 to 1840

1769

Captain James Cook

For over one and a quarter centuries, there was no further recorded contact between the Māori and the Europeans. But in 1769, a naval captain from England, James Cook, returned to the land that was known in English as New Zealand. He and his crew spent many months, and several voyages, exploring the country and making contact with Māori in many areas.

As a result of Cook's explorations, which were big news in Europe and in North America, New Zealand began to be visited by ships from lots of different countries. British, French and American ships hunted whales and seals around its shores. Trading ships also visited, swapping European goods such as blankets, guns and metal tools with food, water, flax and wood traded by local Māori.

1788

the new settlement of Sydney in Australia

In 1788, the British founded the colony of New South Wales in Australia. At that time, they decided that New South Wales should include all the islands they had visited in the South Pacific, so New Zealand became part of New South Wales. Unfortunately, no one asked the Māori people who were already living there. No one from the settlement of Sydney, New South Wales, showed much enthusiasm for actually going to New Zealand either.

1839

Some Māori were tricked into selling their land cheaply.

For 40 years, sailors, whalers, sealers and traders who visited New Zealand did whatever they pleased. There were some Europeans who settled in New Zealand, but there was a lot of lawlessness and bad behaviour.

In 1839, a group of wealthy English businesspeople realised they could make a lot of money by buying land cheaply off the Māori and selling it to English settlers who wanted to start a new life far from England. They formed a company called the New Zealand Company and started selling off land before they'd even bought it. They even started making plans as if they were the government of New Zealand — something that alarmed the real British government, who felt that they should be in charge.

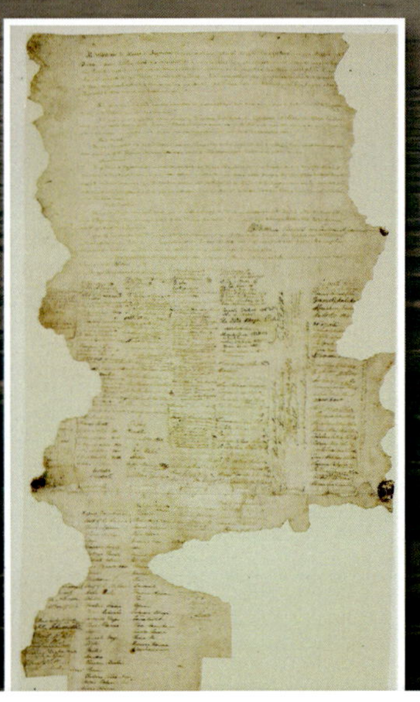

the Treaty of Waitangi, partially burned when the government offices in Auckland caught fire in 1841

On 6 February 1840, the British and about 40 Māori chiefs signed the Treaty of Waitangi, which gave the British government control over New Zealand in return for protecting Māori lands and rights. Despite this, the New Zealand Company continued buying and selling Māori land. They began advertising in England, telling people that they could have a wonderful new life in New Zealand, and that land was cheap and plentiful. For many poor families in England who had little hope of ever owning their own land, this sounded almost too good to be true. Thousands of people signed up to become emigrants. On voyages lasting for months, they sailed halfway around the world in cramped and unhygienic conditions in order to find a better life for themselves and their children.

2 The Logbook of the *Timandra*

The New Zealand Company hired sailing ships to take the emigrants from England to their new land. On 7 September 1841, the cargo ship *Timandra* was chosen as one of these ships, and the owners hurried to make her ready for the voyage. The *Timandra* usually carried coal, wool or other goods, but this time her cargo would be people.

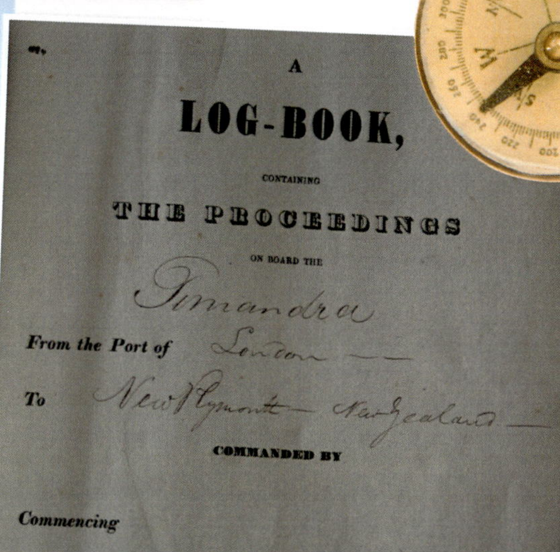

A

LOG-BOOK,

CONTAINING

THE PROCEEDINGS

ON BOARD THE

Timandra

From the Port of London

To New Plymouth — New Zealand

COMMANDED BY

Commencing

Stationer and Chartseller,

High Street.

the Timandra *(left) and ship captain's logbook (above)*

In this book, the voyage of the *Timandra* is recounted by its senior officer, Captain Skinner. Every day, Captain Skinner wrote in his logbook, diarising the events and progress of the journey. Captain Skinner's logbook entries are in green.

A passenger on board, Mr Josiah Flight, also kept a diary. Josiah's diary entries are in blue. In Chapter Three, we hear what settlers thought of their new home, from letters they sent to friends and family back in England.

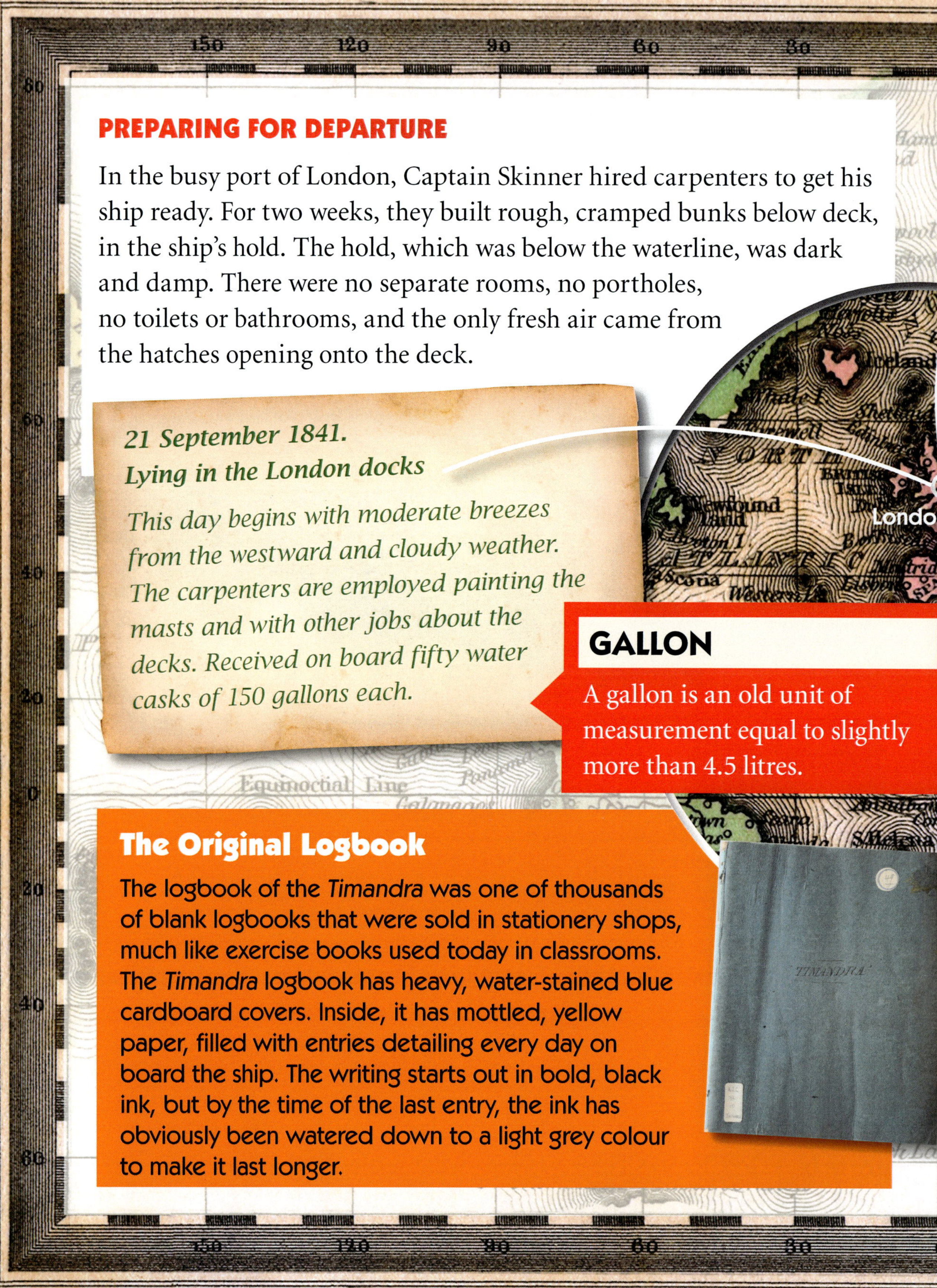

PREPARING FOR DEPARTURE

In the busy port of London, Captain Skinner hired carpenters to get his ship ready. For two weeks, they built rough, cramped bunks below deck, in the ship's hold. The hold, which was below the waterline, was dark and damp. There were no separate rooms, no portholes, no toilets or bathrooms, and the only fresh air came from the hatches opening onto the deck.

21 September 1841.
Lying in the London docks

This day begins with moderate breezes from the westward and cloudy weather. The carpenters are employed painting the masts and with other jobs about the decks. Received on board fifty water casks of 150 gallons each.

GALLON

A gallon is an old unit of measurement equal to slightly more than 4.5 litres.

The Original Logbook

The logbook of the *Timandra* was one of thousands of blank logbooks that were sold in stationery shops, much like exercise books used today in classrooms. The *Timandra* logbook has heavy, water-stained blue cardboard covers. Inside, it has mottled, yellow paper, filled with entries detailing every day on board the ship. The writing starts out in bold, black ink, but by the time of the last entry, the ink has obviously been watered down to a light grey colour to make it last longer.

7 October 1841.
Lying in the London docks

This day begins with moderate breezes and cloudy weather. The crew is employed boarding the sails and hauling the ship to another jetty to take on board the anchors and their cables. Took in several of the stores this day.

SHIP'S STORES

The ship's stores consisted of the food that would be taken on the voyage. The chart below shows the amounts of different foods the New Zealand Company allowed Captain Skinner to take on board to feed the emigrants.

Food Stores for 212 Emigrants for Four Months	
Bread 9 100 kilograms	Potatoes 3 930 kilograms
Beef 1 300 kilograms	Tea 80 kilograms
Pork 1 960 kilograms	Coffee 120 kilograms
Preserved meat 1 300 kilograms	Sugar 980 kilograms
Flour 2 290 kilograms	Butter 490 kilograms
Raisins 650 kilograms	Pickled cabbage 430 litres
Suet 240 kilograms	Salt 160 kilograms
Peas 2 090 litres	Mustard 40 kilograms
Rice 1 300 kilograms	

In addition, the captain was allowed to take medical supplies, which consisted of 280 litres of lime juice (to ward off scurvy), 60 kilograms of oatmeal and five kilograms of arrowroot.

MEAL TIME

The New Zealand Company had decided exactly when and what the emigrants would be fed during their voyage. For breakfast and dinner, they would only be allowed tea or coffee and some sugar. There would only be one meal a day, in the afternoon.

11 October 1841.
From London to Gravesend

This day began with fresh breezes from the westward. At three o'clock, the sailing order came on board from the New Zealand Company. Two pilots came on board and took the ship to Gravesend, all the crew on board. Came into the lower part of Gravesend beach in seven fathoms of water.

PILOTS

Pilots are people experienced in navigating ships through difficult areas. The twisting and busy River Thames was one of these areas, and ships needed pilots to guide them from London to the open sea.

Nautical Measurements

Seafarers have always measured distances and depths in different ways to people on land. A fathom was a unit of measurement that was originally the span of a person's outstretched arms. Later it was standardised to equal a depth of 1.8 metres. Another nautical measurement is the knot, which is a speed of 1.9 kilometres per hour. The name comes from the knotted rope that was let out behind a ship to measure its speed. The crew let the rope pass over the stern as the ship moved, and counted the number of knots in the rope that passed in a given time. Leagues were measures of distance relating to how far a person, horse or rowboat could travel in an hour. At sea, a league was about 5.6 kilometres.

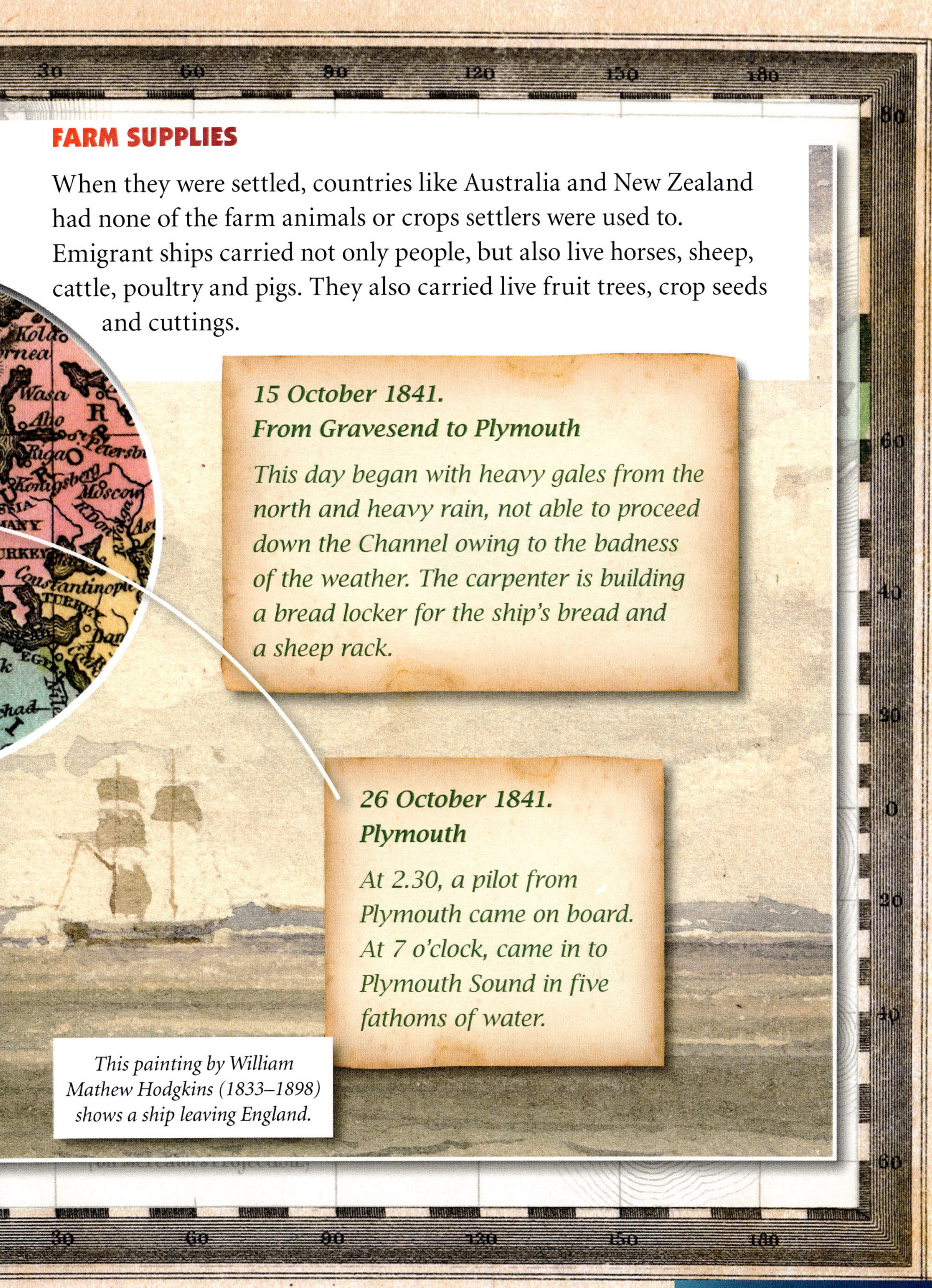

FARM SUPPLIES

When they were settled, countries like Australia and New Zealand had none of the farm animals or crops settlers were used to. Emigrant ships carried not only people, but also live horses, sheep, cattle, poultry and pigs. They also carried live fruit trees, crop seeds and cuttings.

15 October 1841.
From Gravesend to Plymouth

This day began with heavy gales from the north and heavy rain, not able to proceed down the Channel owing to the badness of the weather. The carpenter is building a bread locker for the ship's bread and a sheep rack.

26 October 1841.
Plymouth

At 2.30, a pilot from Plymouth came on board. At 7 o'clock, came in to Plymouth Sound in five fathoms of water.

This painting by William Mathew Hodgkins (1833–1898) shows a ship leaving England.

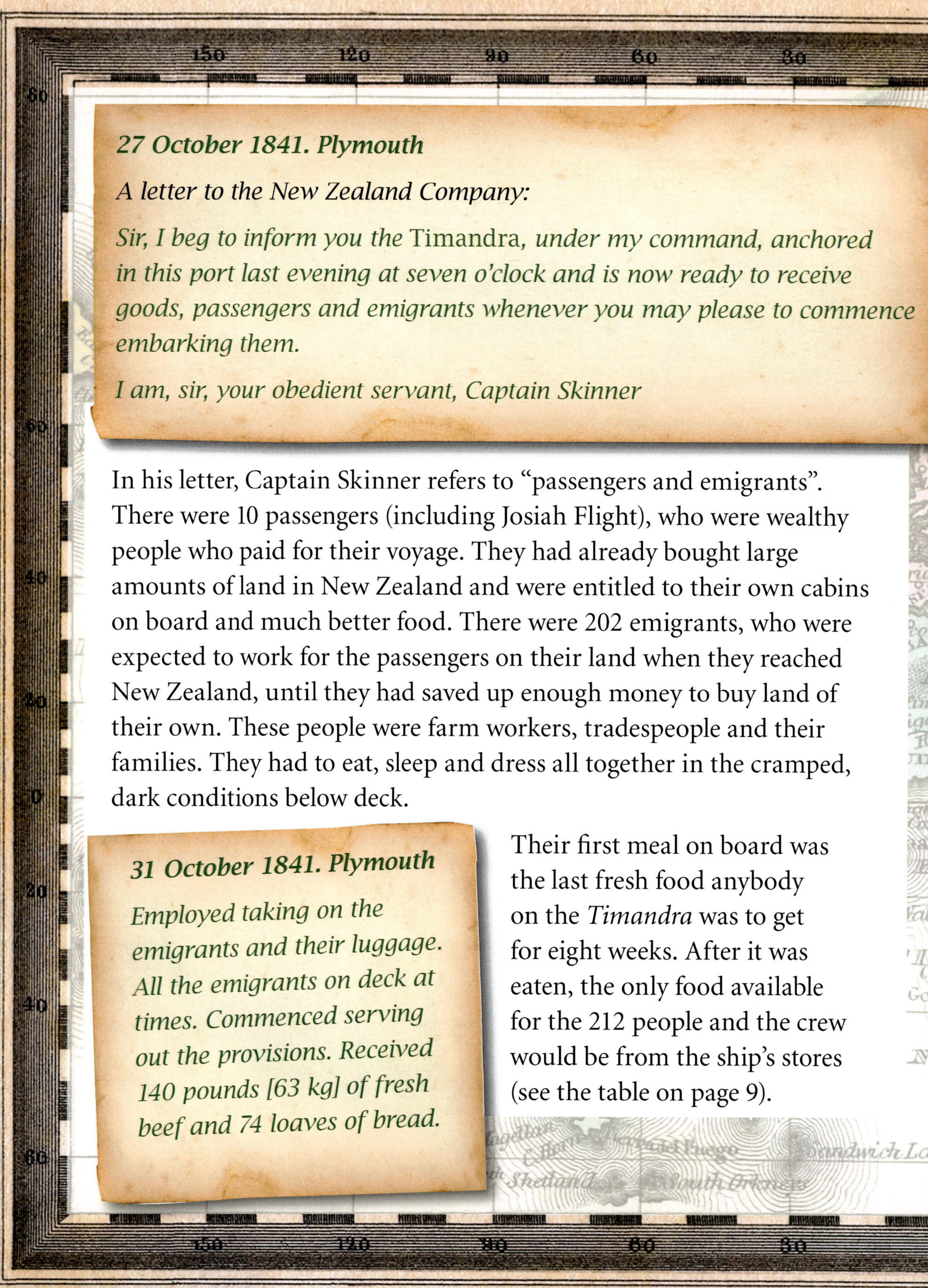

27 October 1841. Plymouth

A letter to the New Zealand Company:

Sir, I beg to inform you the Timandra, *under my command, anchored in this port last evening at seven o'clock and is now ready to receive goods, passengers and emigrants whenever you may please to commence embarking them.*

I am, sir, your obedient servant, Captain Skinner

In his letter, Captain Skinner refers to "passengers and emigrants". There were 10 passengers (including Josiah Flight), who were wealthy people who paid for their voyage. They had already bought large amounts of land in New Zealand and were entitled to their own cabins on board and much better food. There were 202 emigrants, who were expected to work for the passengers on their land when they reached New Zealand, until they had saved up enough money to buy land of their own. These people were farm workers, tradespeople and their families. They had to eat, sleep and dress all together in the cramped, dark conditions below deck.

31 October 1841. Plymouth

Employed taking on the emigrants and their luggage. All the emigrants on deck at times. Commenced serving out the provisions. Received 140 pounds [63 kg] of fresh beef and 74 loaves of bread.

Their first meal on board was the last fresh food anybody on the *Timandra* was to get for eight weeks. After it was eaten, the only food available for the 212 people and the crew would be from the ship's stores (see the table on page 9).

1 November 1841. Plymouth

Mustered all the emigrants on the poop and took a list of names, being 202 and ten passengers.

This nineteenth-century engraving shows English emigrants embarking for their journey.

3 November 1841. From Plymouth to New Zealand

This day began with moderate breezes from the southwest and clear weather. At two o'clock, got underway from Plymouth Sound, all the emigrants and passengers on board. At midnight, ship pitching heavily and shipping much water in the forecastle.

4 November 1841.

A nasty head sea, ship pitching heavily. All the emigrants below deck being seasick.

7 November 1841.

All the emigrants on deck, and the 'tween decks cleaned, all well on board. One of the emigrants gave birth to a fine child, both doing well. Latitude 41° N.

A Seafarer's Glossary

Seafarers have special names for different parts of a ship:

Aft the rear part of the ship
Bow the forward part of the hull
Fore the front part of the ship
Forecastle or **fo'c'sle** the front deck, in front of the mast
Gunwale the raised fence around the edge of the ship
Hull the outer frame and wooden skin of the ship
Poop Deck the rear deck, built over the top of the cabin
Stern the rear part of the hull
'Tween Decks the space between the decks of a ship

In addition, they use **port** and **starboard** instead of "left" and "right". When facing the bow, "port" means "left", and "starboard" means "right".

"All the emigrants on deck ..." (7 November 1841)

The seas around Europe were busy, and ships had to take care not to collide.

Latitude

Latitudes are imaginary lines drawn on a map to mark how far north or south something is. Seafarers calculated their latitude by measuring the height above the horizon of certain stars. The equator, which is the imaginary line that runs around the middle of Earth, is at latitude 0° (0 degrees). The North Pole is at latitude 90° N (90 degrees North). The South Pole is at latitude 90° S (90 degrees South). The *Timandra* started her journey at latitude 51° N. Her destination, New Plymouth, was at latitude 39° S.

INFANT MORTALITY

In the nineteenth century, out of every 1 000 babies born, around 15 would be born already dead, or stillborn. In the twenty-first century in countries with good healthcare systems, this has been reduced to one in 10 000.

9 November 1841. Latitude 36° N

Passing squalls of rain. At seven o'clock, one of the emigrants gave birth to a stillborn child.

Remember Captain Skinner's logbook entries are in green, and Josiah Flight's letters are in blue.

13 November 1841.

Weather fine, sighted vessels in morning, all left astern, out of sight by noon. Opened cases of trees; found them healthy; buds swelling. Cabin passengers held a consultation on the conduct of the emigrants (language; coming on Poop deck); also as to starting school for the children. Agreed to form ourselves into a committee for superintending school. Dr. Forbes to draw up a Proclamation covering behaviour, etc.

36°N

5°N

14 November 1841.

Church service at half-past 10 a.m. Many of the emigrants offended at not being allowed use of the Poop deck, would not attend. Awning spread over Poop deck.

16 November 1841.

An emigrant who had offered to assist us in the school came to say that he was sorry he could not have anything to do with it, as it was contrary to the wish of the other emigrants, and he did not feel himself at liberty to act contrary to their wishes. The emigrants did not like the interference of the cabin passengers, who only wished to have the credit of conducting the school whilst the others did all the work. The school was opened at 11 a.m., eight of the emigrants assisting.

25 November 1841.
Latitude 5° N

Clear, pleasant weather. All the emigrants on deck this day, 'tween decks cleaned and sprinkled with chloride of lime. The children at school four hours in this day.

CHLORIDE OF LIME

Captain Skinner of the *Timandra* was expected to sprinkle a powder called chloride of lime throughout the ship every day. Chloride of lime is an antiseptic, designed to kill bacteria and microbes that might cause disease. It is a strong-smelling mixture of chlorine (the chemical added to swimming pools to keep them clean) and lime, which is a caustic powder that can burn the eyes and skin.

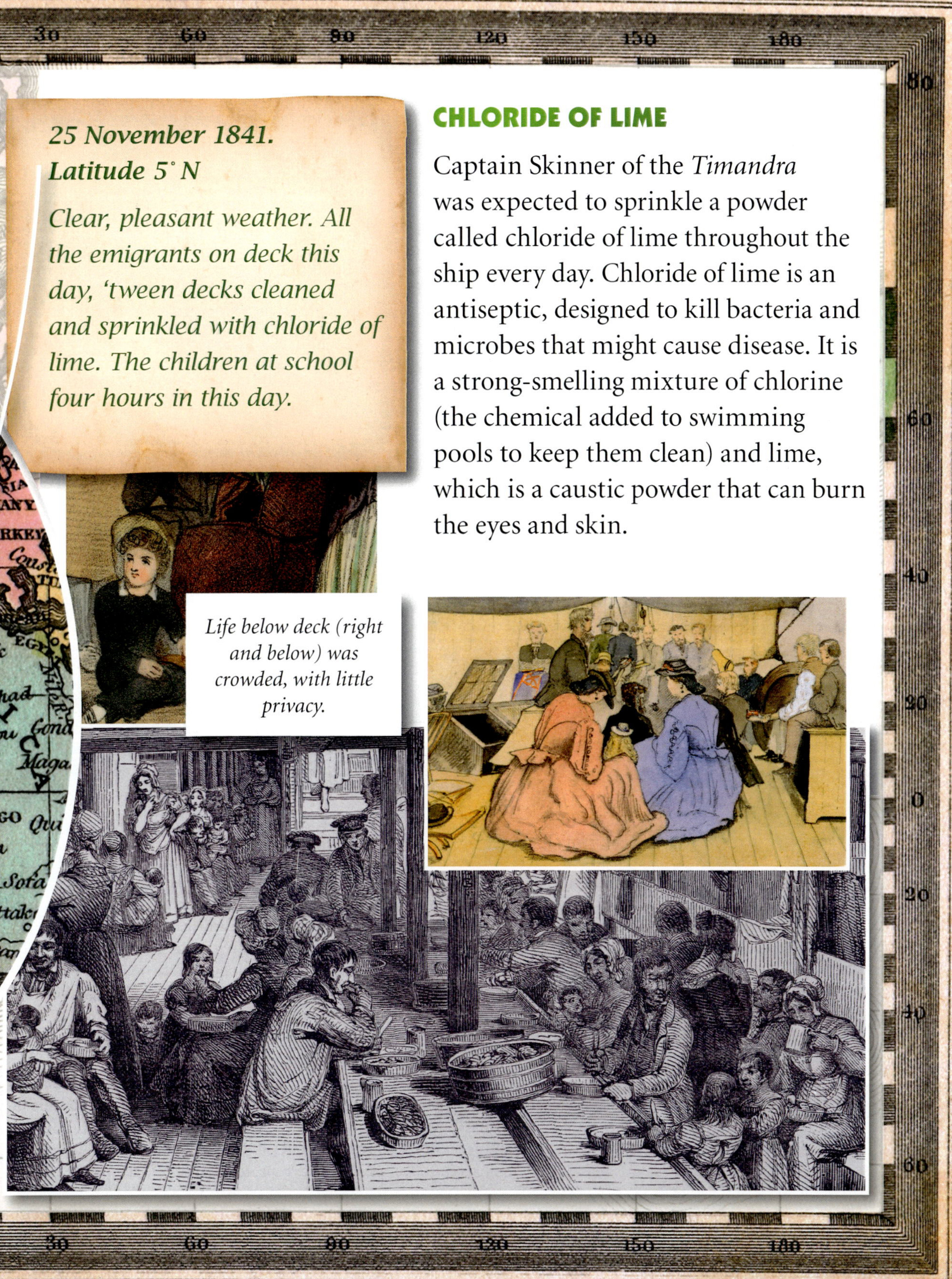

Life below deck (right and below) was crowded, with little privacy.

26 November 1841.

Weather squally with rain. Whilst at tea the weather changed from a calm to such a stiff breeze suddenly, that the Captain jumped up from the table and in a few minutes got the ship under stormsail under which we drove for the night. The rain came down in torrents.

29 November 1841.
Latitude 0°

Fire stoves lighted to dry the deck. At three o'clock an infant belonging to one of the emigrants died, age three weeks (see entry for 7 November 1841).

4 December 1841.
Latitude 14° S

Mr O'Neill, one of the emigrants, complained of the badness of the water, but it was proved by the surgeon, Captain and all the passengers that there was not any fault in it.

The water had been brought on board in wooden casks on 21 September, over 13 weeks previously.

6 December 1841.
Latitude 19° S

Clear, pleasant weather. At three o'clock, a child belonging to one of the emigrants died aged two years.

11 December 1841.
Latitude 28° S

At midnight, steady breezes and clear weather. At four o'clock, same weather, a child belonging to one of the emigrants died, aged two years. At eight o'clock, steady breezes and clear weather.

14 December 1841.
Latitude 31° S

At five o'clock, Doctor Forbes buried a child belonging to one of the emigrants, aged three years and a half. Moderate winds and cloudy weather.

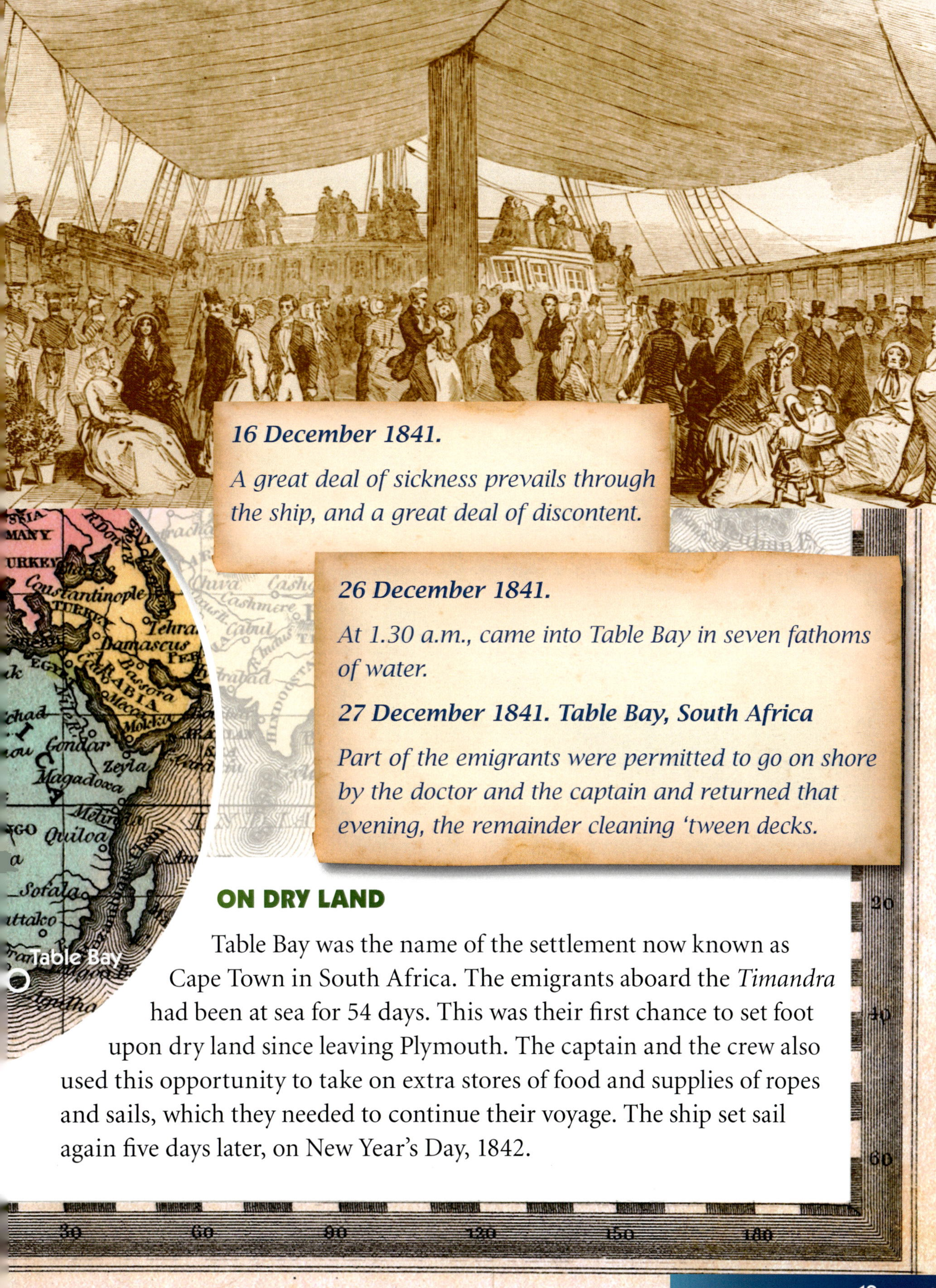

16 December 1841.

A great deal of sickness prevails through the ship, and a great deal of discontent.

26 December 1841.

At 1.30 a.m., came into Table Bay in seven fathoms of water.

27 December 1841. Table Bay, South Africa

Part of the emigrants were permitted to go on shore by the doctor and the captain and returned that evening, the remainder cleaning 'tween decks.

ON DRY LAND

Table Bay was the name of the settlement now known as Cape Town in South Africa. The emigrants aboard the *Timandra* had been at sea for 54 days. This was their first chance to set foot upon dry land since leaving Plymouth. The captain and the crew also used this opportunity to take on extra stores of food and supplies of ropes and sails, which they needed to continue their voyage. The ship set sail again five days later, on New Year's Day, 1842.

LIFE BELOW DECKS

In his diary, Dr George Forbes, the doctor on the *Timandra*, described the scene below decks as "a little [place] of swearing, filth, theft and pilfering". He also wrote that the emigrants had a tendency to "do nothing from morn till night but make puddings, compositions of bacon and fat, eat and cook, eternally eating, cooking and baking. Some nearly killed themselves and their children by downright cramming."

12 January 1842.
Latitude 38° S

Several of the emigrants returned their cans of preserved meat, being sour and not fit to be eaten. Gave others in here to them.

18 January 1842.
Latitude 40° S

By using the moon, stars and the sun, I have arrived at our longitude which is 48° E.

6 February 1842.
Latitude 44° S

Opened a cask of sugar, which was refused by the emigrants being sandy, and a dark colour.

LONGITUDE

Longitude is a description of how far east or west a place is from Greenwich in London, England, using imaginary lines similar to latitude. Greenwich is at 0° longitude. Before radio and electronic navigation aids, calculating it was extremely difficult, as precise measurements of the moon, sun and the stars had to be made, often in rough conditions at sea. These measurements were then compared to charts that showed where the moon, sun and stars were expected to be. Seafarers also had to know the exact time. At dawn on 18 January 1842, Captain Skinner could observe for the only time the moon, sun and stars together. This meant it was the only time during the entire voyage that he actually knew exactly where his ship was.

11 February 1842. Latitude 44° S

Chloride of lime is to be sprinkled every day throughout the passage to keep away all disease from the ship. At ten in the evening, I went down 'tween decks with the doctor to see the chloride of lime sprinkled, which some of the emigrants said should not be done as it burned their clothes. I immediately took the bucket and commenced sprinkling the chloride over the decks. One of the emigrants seized hold of my collar and threw me down on the deck. For this offence, I, Captain Skinner, had him put in irons on the poop for twenty-four hours until he thought proper to beg pardon and keep the peace for the remainder of the passage.

NAUTICAL LAW AND PUNISHMENT

On board a ship, the captain is responsible for making sure everyone obeys the law, and everyone must obey the captain's commands. In the nineteenth century, punishments for not obeying the captain included being locked up with iron shackles around your ankles or wrists ("put in irons"), being whipped or, in some cases, being thrown overboard.

31° S

Table Bay

The emigrant's version of the events of 11 February was different. He stated that his wife was lying ill on the bed when a sailor, whose duty it was to deal with their cabin, told her to get up. When she failed to do so the sailor went to pull the bedclothes off her. This was too much for the emigrant, who knocked the sailor down. The sailor then brought the captain to the scene and when the emigrant was splashed with lime, he knocked the captain down too. A terrific struggle with several of the crew took place before he was restrained in irons as the captain ordered.

Seafarers' Words and Commands

Ahoy used to draw attention to something, for example "boat ahoy" or "land ahoy"

All hands the entire crew aboard a ship

Avast a command to stop doing whatever is being done

Aye, aye said to show that someone has heard a command and will carry it out

Batten down the hatches a command to nail pieces of wood over the hatches during a storm

Bitter end a bitt is a post to which the anchor rope is tied, so when the anchor has dropped to the full length of the rope, things are at the "bitter end"

Cat out of the bag a whip used for punishments was called a cat-o'-nine-tails and when it was about to be used, seafarers said the "cat was out of the bag". This meant something was about to happen.

Know the ropes a seafarer who knew all the ropes on board a ship was very experienced

Slush fund "slush" was the greasy leftovers from barrels of preserved meat, which was sold by the cook as a lubricant for ropes and pulleys. The money he made was called his "slush fund".

Weigh anchor to haul the anchor up

13 February 1842. 43° S

At seven o'clock in the evening, the southwest cape of Van Diemen's Land bore north-by-northwest at a distance of fifteen or sixteen leagues.

22 February 1842. Arrived at New Plymouth, New Zealand

At noon, hard gales, squally weather, we stood to the south-west of the islands off the coast, three or four leagues off shore, deeming it not prudent to run into the bay.

24 February 1842.

Large whale-boat came off for emigrants; The people on shore were living in tents, huts formed of reeds or mud, and a few in one-storeyed houses. Put up tent. Strong breeze from south-east.

24 February 1842.

This day begins with moderate breezes and clear, pleasant weather. Sent the emigrants on shore this day. They were victualled for this day, making 117 days they have been victualled on board this ship.

26 February 1842.

Weather beautifully fine. Eight boatloads of goods landed. Slept in tent. Rather rough. Fleas and sandflies abound. Rats innumerable. Landed sheep.

After arrival (left), emigrants were rowed ashore to huts (below).

THE LAST FREE MEAL

Being "victualled" meant being fed. This was the last free meal the emigrants received. Their long, cramped voyage to a new home was over. They were rowed to the shore, along with their luggage. Temporary accommodation in huts made from reeds and ferns was available in the tiny settlement of New Plymouth, New Zealand. The emigrants had to find work within a day or two of coming ashore in their new homeland – otherwise, they and their families would starve.

THE END OF THE VOYAGE

Captain Skinner set about readying his ship, the *Timandra*, for another voyage and a few weeks later he received the following letter.

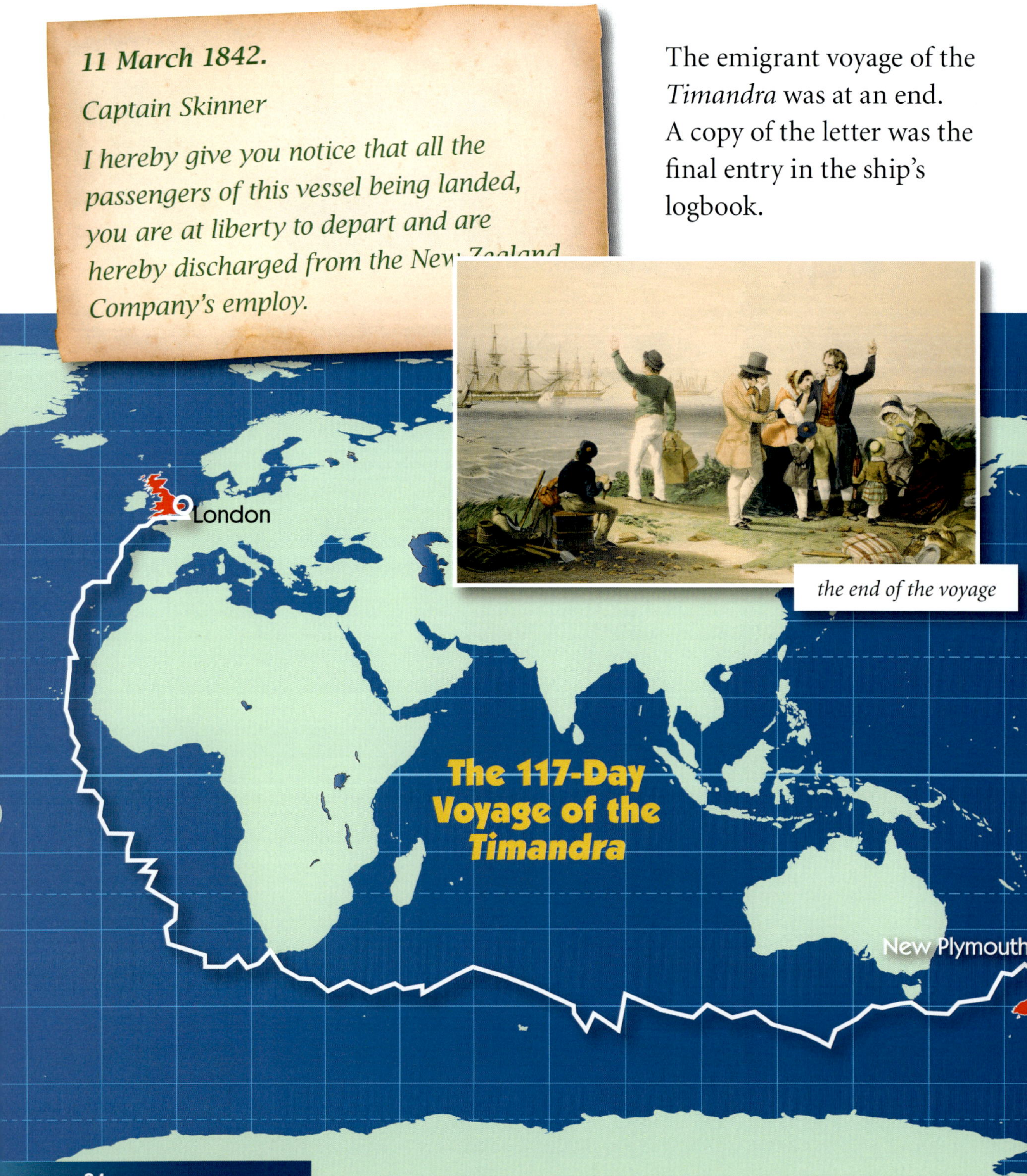

11 March 1842.

Captain Skinner

I hereby give you notice that all the passengers of this vessel being landed, you are at liberty to depart and are hereby discharged from the New Zealand Company's employ.

The emigrant voyage of the *Timandra* was at an end. A copy of the letter was the final entry in the ship's logbook.

the end of the voyage

3 Letters Home

A few days after landing, one of the emigrants, Stephen Gillingham, wrote a letter home to his father in England, describing his experiences. He wrote:

I take the opportunity of writing to inform you of our safe arrival. We came to an anchor on February 23rd, about three miles from the shore, at 4 o'clock p.m. hoisted the English colours, and fired a salute of two six-pounders [cannons], which was answered in a few minutes from the shore. The next morning the boats came off, and during the day all the passengers and their luggage were landed. Every one of the emigrants got employment immediately on their landing at 5/- per day, carpenters 7/6. They have taken houses at 5/- to 15/- per week. I would advise all persons coming hither to marry first, as the bachelors seem to be in want of housekeepers. The town is situated between two small rivers, both of which abound with mountain trout and eels, and their waters are as good as any I have ever tasted.

It is a beautiful country, abundantly supplied with water and wood.

the settlement of New Plymouth, 1842

See page 26 for an explanation of the money of the time.

Letters that the emigrants wrote home to their friends and families give us the best sense of how they felt about their new homeland. The following is a collection of some other letters that emigrants wrote home.

Dear Father

We have grown fine wheat and barley here, the finest that you ever saw, very fine; and new potatoes and turnips on Christmas day for dinner. Henry and Charles go to school. Henry is just learning to write, the schoolmaster is just newly set up; it is 6d. a week for Charles, and 9d. a week for Henry; he has been at writing some weeks. Dear father, when you voyage here, please bring me out a barrel of pilchards; please buy a gardening hook too. There are plenty of mackerel here, but no nets to catch them, and there are pilchards; please to bring one good pilchard net.

From JANE CROCKER to her father, 10 February 1842.

a watercolour view of New Plymouth, 1842

MONEY – POUNDS, SHILLINGS AND PENNIES

The emigrants used English money, which at that time was divided into pounds, shillings and pennies. A shilling (or 1/- as it was written) was worth about ten cents. Six pennies (or 6d. as it was written) was equivalent to about 5 cents. Therefore, as mentioned in Stephen Gillingham's letter on page 25, most emigrants got work on fifty cents a day; and according to the letter above, it cost around five cents a week to send a child to school.

Dear Father, Brother and Sisters

I write you these few lines hoping it will find you all well. I have been expecting to hear from you before now, as there have been three ships come here from England since I left. We have a small harvest, as we had no time, when we came, to sow much, and no cattle to plough the ground. We have got plenty of potatoes, fine crops, and fine cabbages. I wish you were all here. This is a fine place for tailors and sawyers. I can get more money here than you can get at home. I am certain I should never have saved as much at home.

Love to all friends, from your affectionate children,

SAMUEL AND F. CURTIS, New Plymouth, 10 February 1842.

"Sawyers" are people who saw wood for a living.

Dear Mother

This I hope will find you all in good health, as it leaves me at present. My family, Thomas and James are all well; we have buried our dear little baby; nine weeks old when he died. We had a long voyage; our family was not on land, after we went on board at Plymouth, until landed here at New Plymouth, six months and three days on board.

WILLIAM BAYLY, New Plymouth, 29 February 1842.

Dear Father and Mother

Please give my love to brothers and sisters, and tell them I should be happy to see them here as quick as possible. If they come, they should bring as much clothes, shoes, and bedding as they can, as it is all very dear here; they should also bring a good gun or two, as wild ducks and pigeons are very plentiful here; likewise some apple pips or kernels in earth, and all kinds of herb seeds, as no such thing is to be got here, and the land is very rich and climate temperate. Any crop is brought to perfection here in half the time it is in England. Please to give my kind love to all inquiring friends, and tell them we are looking very well. We are very healthy and happy, and we say we never wish to return to England.

SIMON and JANE ANDREWS, New Plymouth, 8 March 1842.

My dear brother Robert,

I don't think that there would be many return to England if free passages were given them.

P.S. Send out a watch and clock maker, for all the clocks and watches are stopped, and no person here is able to repair them. And above all things use your diligence in sending a hair dresser, for all the gentlemen are perfect frights because their hair is so long; they look more like women then men, not having had their hair cut since they left England.

S. GILLINGHAM, New Plymouth, 1 October 1842.

This letter is from the writer of the letter on page 25.

My dear Sir,

There are no large houses or stores, but the country is dotted over with pretty cottages; and the shopkeepers are now selling a variety of useful and desirable articles at reasonable prices.

The price of flour at present is 3 1/2d. a pound by the bag or barrel, and fresh pork 7d. a pound. Mutton is rarely brought to market, but sheep have been lambing this season. Fish is frequently caught and sold at 3d. per pound or less. The best are the rock-cod, eels and crayfish. Besides these are the snapper, baracouta and other kinds, common to most waters in New Zealand. From the south, we have obtained working oxen and cows; and in the course of next summer we expect a large increase of cattle overland. At present fresh butter and milk from cows are scarce, but there are plenty of goats.

J. T. WICKSTEED, New Plymouth, 23 November 1842.

Dear Thomas,

The Essex got safely here on the 20th instant; two births and one death; the latter, that of an infant, at Port Nicholson. This vessel came to us in remarkably good condition. The captain and surgeon must have done their duty well. Nearly all the children took the scarlet fever, and all recovered.

UNKNOWN, New Plymouth, 24 January 1843.

SCARLET FEVER

In the cramped and damp conditions below deck, illness and disease were common. Scarlet fever is a bacterial infection that gives its victims a very sore throat, a high temperature, a painful rash, and a very red tongue and throat. Before antibiotics were discovered, many people died of simple bacterial infections such as this.

Dear Aunt

There is a great deal of talk about a girl in town who is going to marry a very handsome young Maori – indeed, the nicest looking man of any sort we have seen here. Her name is Mary Bishop and she does not bear a very good character. She fell in love with and popped the question to the young man! If this match comes off, it will be the first instance here of a white woman marrying a Maori, although there have been several the other way.

MARY HIRST, New Plymouth, 1843.

Read page 31 to find out what happened to Mary Bishop!

two panoramic views of the settlement's growth in the 1840s

4 The Emigrants' Legacy

Good Times and Bad

Between 1841 and 1843, six ships brought emigrants to the small settlement of New Plymouth.

They carried 1 012 passengers: 896 emigrants and 116 "passengers" who mostly paid their own way. Almost three quarters of the emigrants came from Devon and Cornwall in England.

The first few years of New Plymouth must have seemed idyllic for the new emigrants. Almost all of them were allocated land to farm and build houses upon, and most of them managed to save enough money to eventually buy that land.

But, as the town grew and the population swelled, the New Zealand Company and other people, eager to get rich quick, used English law to force the local Māori tribes out of more and more of their lands. By March 1860, the British government and the local Māori tribes were at war.

a battle during the war of 1860–61

Over 3 500 soldiers were brought from Australia. For a year, neither side achieved a victory. Eventually, in 1861, the fighting stopped. Many of the settlers, who had become friends with the local Māori, had opposed the fighting. They were disappointed that the tribes that had welcomed them to their new homes had been treated unfairly.

Today, New Plymouth is a city with over 70 000 people. It is a city that is proud of its heritage and of the people – both Māori and British – who worked together in the early 1840s to build its foundations. Many of the street signs and localities in New Plymouth bear the names of the settlers or the towns and villages they came from. And people are especially proud if one of their ancestors was on board one of the six emigrant ships that brought the first settlers to this part of the world – even if that ancestor was an emigrant called Mary Bishop, who did not "bear a very good character" and asked a handsome young Māori man to marry her.

THAT GIRL, WHO LIVED TO BE 78 YEARS OLD, WAS MY GREAT-GREAT-GREAT-GRANDMOTHER.

John Parsons, author

the modern city of New Plymouth

Index

Glossary

astern Behind the ship

colonisation The settling of another country by a foreign nation

colony A group of people who settle in another region but maintain connection with, and follow the laws of, their original land

emigrant Somebody who leaves their homeland to live somewhere else

logbook The official record that a ship's captain keeps of the voyage

nautical Relating to sailing or ships

squalls Sudden strong winds that quickly die away

vessel Any craft that travels on water